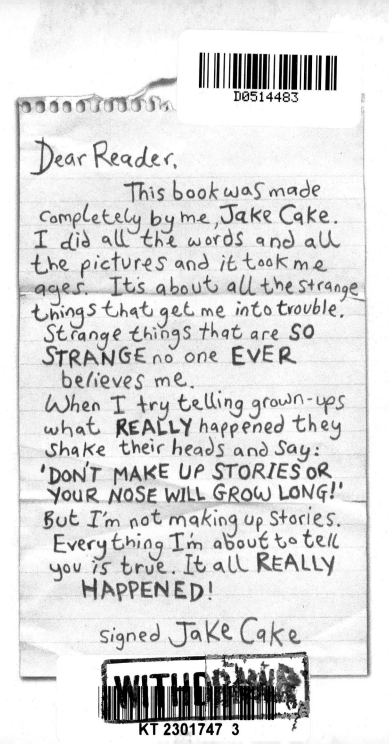

Dear Reader,

This book was made completely by me, Jake Cake. I did all the words and all the pictures and it took me ages. It's about all the strange things that get me into trouble. Strange things that are SO STRANGE no one EVER believes me.

When I try telling grown-ups what REALLY happened they shake their heads and say: 'DON'T MAKE UP STORIES OR YOUR NOSE WILL GROW LONG!'

But I'm not making up stories. Everything I'm about to tell you is true. It all REALLY HAPPENED!

signed Jake Cake

Michael Broad spent much of his childhood gazing out of the window imagining he was somewhere more interesting.

Now he's a grown-up Michael still spends a lot of time gazing out of the window imagining he's somewhere more interesting – but now he writes and illustrates books as well.

Some of them are picture books, like *Broken Bird* and *The Little Star Who Wished*.

michaelbroad.co.uk

Books by Michael Broad

JAKE CAKE: THE FOOTBALL BEAST
JAKE CAKE: THE PIRATE CURSE
JAKE CAKE: THE ROBOT DINNER LADY
JAKE CAKE: THE SCHOOL DRAGON
JAKE CAKE: THE VISITING VAMPIRE
JAKE CAKE: THE WEREWOLF TEACHER

JAKE CAKE
THE SCHOOL DRAGON

MICHAEL BROAD

PUFFIN

This book is dedicated to my friend Ann

PUFFIN BOOKS

Published by the Penguin Group
Penguin Books Ltd, 80 Strand, London WC2R 0RL, England
Penguin Group (USA) Inc., 375 Hudson Street, New York, New York 10014, USA
Penguin Group (Canada), 90 Eglinton Avenue East, Suite 700, Toronto, Ontario, Canada M4P 2Y3
(a division of Pearson Penguin Canada Inc.)
Penguin Ireland, 25 St Stephen's Green, Dublin 2, Ireland (a division of Penguin Books Ltd)
Penguin Group (Australia), 250 Camberwell Road, Camberwell, Victoria 3124, Australia
(a division of Pearson Australia Group Pty Ltd)
Penguin Books India Pvt Ltd, 11 Community Centre, Panchsheel Park, New Delhi – 110 017, India
Penguin Group (NZ), 67 Apollo Drive, Rosedale, North Shore 0632, New Zealand
(a division of Pearson New Zealand Ltd)
Penguin Books (South Africa) (Pty) Ltd, 24 Sturdee Avenue, Rosebank, Johannesburg 2196, South Africa

Penguin Books Ltd, Registered Offices: 80 Strand, London WC2R 0RL, England

puffinbooks.com

First published 2007
007

Set in Perpetua by Palimpsest Book Production Limited,
Grangemouth, Stirlingshire
Made and printed in England by Clays Ltd, St Ives plc

British Library Cataloguing in Publication Data
A CIP catalogue record for this book is available from the British Library

ISBN: 978-0-141-32089-2

www.greenpenguin.co.uk

MIX
Paper from
responsible sources
FSC FSC® C018179

Penguin Books is committed to a sustainable
future for our business, our readers and our planet.
This book is made from Forest Stewardship
Council™ certified paper.

Here are three UNBELIEVABLE
stories about the
times I met:

Mrs Grump looked up from the
register, craned her neck and
scanned the classroom like a submarine
periscope looking for enemy ships. She
fixed her sights on me and immediately
frowned. From the look on her face I

could tell my
teacher wanted
to launch torpedoes
at me from under her desk.
But I couldn't be in trouble *already* —
the register hadn't even been called yet!

Mrs Grump's frown quickly turned
into a glare and then she
began tapping herself
angrily on the head! I was
beginning to think my
form teacher had gone
a bit mad, when

she rolled her eyes, stormed across the classroom and plucked the woolly hat from my head. 'Well?' she growled. 'Are you *here* or are you *not* here?'

'Oh,' I said, realizing I hadn't heard my name being called because of the hat pulled over my ears. 'I'm here!' I added cheerily.

'And you can take that off too!' she snapped, pointing to

the scarf wrapped snugly around my neck. 'You're not in the playground any more.'

'But it's *freezing*, Mrs Grump!' I whined, and I wasn't just whining for the fun of it. It was so cold in the classroom I was expecting to see polar bears and penguins shuffle in for the register!

Mrs Grump must have realized I had a point because she raised a curious eyebrow, licked her finger and waved it in the air.

'Hmmm,' she said, stepping over to the nearest radiator. Mrs Grump tapped the top cautiously and then pressed her hand firmly against it.

'Hmmm,' she said again, as though considering all the evidence.

Mrs Grump returned to my desk and shoved the woolly hat back on my head.

'As you seem to be the most suitably dressed, you can run along to the basement and ask Mr Knight why we appear to be without heat this morning,' she said firmly.

SHOVE!

And she didn't have to ask twice!
I wasn't going to miss a chance to
escape lessons, so I legged it out of the
classroom and down the corridor before
Mrs Grump could change her mind.

I was also keen to see the basement
because everyone said it was haunted!

I didn't believe it was haunted. I
suspected it was probably just full of
mops and buckets and other boring
caretaker things. But, opening the
creaky old basement door and peering
down the dark stone steps, I began to
have second thoughts.

Especially when I heard a great big
GROAN in the distance!

GULP!

Ghosts *are* well known for groaning – groaning and rattling chains (I once had an encounter with a ghost who liked rattling toilet chains, but I'll tell you about that another time).

GROAN!

This time something told me the groan hadn't come from a groaning ghost. It rumbled and made my teeth rattle, which meant whatever was groaning in the basement was something really, really BIG!

I suppose I could have legged it back to class, but then everyone would think I was scared of the haunted basement, and I couldn't have them thinking that. So I carried on down the steps and hoped I'd find the caretaker *before* I found the mysterious BIG THING — and *definitely* before the mysterious BIG THING found me!

'Mr Knight?' I called, reaching the bottom step and peering into the gloomy basement.

The place was like a large underground cave with huge brick pillars (that were probably holding the school up), and stacks of old chairs and desks (that a BIG THING could easily hide behind!). So I kept my eyes peeled and crept along slowly, pausing whenever I thought I heard something.

The groaning seemed to have stopped – which meant I'd either imagined it or the BIG THING was hiding somewhere and waiting to pounce. So I was relieved when I finally found the caretaker's office, even though it was empty. But at least I could go back to class and say

Mr Knight wasn't there and no one
would think I was a big scaredy cat!

PHEW!

GROOOOAAAAAN!

GULP!

The groan was right behind me.
Which meant the BIG THING stood
between me, and my only way out

GROAN!  of the basement! I was trapped! Taking a deep breath I turned round slowly and stared into two huge yellow eyes. The huge yellow eyes of a dragon!

You might be wondering how I could be certain it was a dragon, especially as I'd never seen one before. But when you see your first dragon there's no doubting what it is. This one was big and red and scaly, it had wings on its back, massive claws and a spiky tail.

Oh, and it also had black smoke billowing from its nostrils!

DEFINITELY a dragon!
'ARRRRRGGGGH!' I
screamed at the top of my voice.

Screaming at the top of your voice isn't the most practical thing to do when confronted with a dragon, but it seemed like the right thing to do at the time.

The dragon's huge eyes suddenly grew wider, then it clasped its front feet over its ears and with a high-pitched yelp it thundered away, deeper into the basement!

PHEW!

Now the exit was clear I ran as fast as

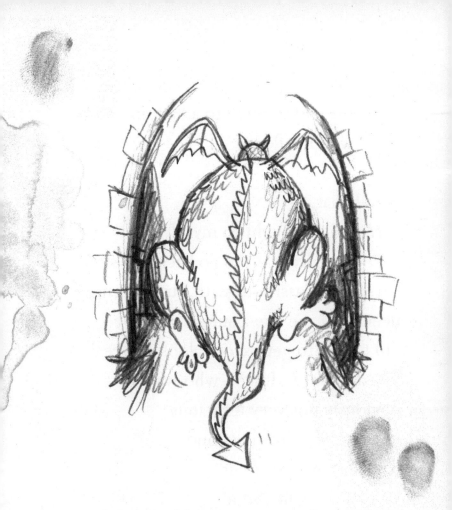

my legs would carry me, up the stone
steps two at a time and out into the
corridor. I was halfway back to Mrs
Grump's classroom when I stopped

suddenly and skidded to a halt on the shiny wooden floor.

I scratched my head through the woolly hat.

Hmmm, I thought to myself.

Did I really want to go back and sit in a freezing classroom with Mrs Grump peering at me like a submarine? Or did I want to get a closer look at a real live dragon? A dragon who was obviously not very ferocious if it ran away from *me*, and it wasn't even *that* big when I thought about it – not for a dragon anyway.

Hmmm, I thought again,

SCRATCH
"SCRATCH"
"SCRATCH"

considering all the evidence.

Then I crept back down into the
basement.

I immediately heard the groaning
again, although now it was groaning

and sniffing, which isn't anywhere near as scary as just groaning. Following the sound, I eventually found the great red scaly heap shivering in the furthest corner of the basement.

The dragon was lying on a bed of straw that I noticed was a bit singed in places. Two sad yellow eyes peered out at me from the shadows like a

frightened puppy (but obviously a
massive puppy with huge scales instead
of fur).

'There, there,' I whispered, moving
slowly forward. 'Good dragon.'

I reached out my hand to
pat the dragon's head when
suddenly it leapt up without
warning. The dragon arched
its back and flicked
open its massive
wings, then it
took a great

Pat
Pat

lungful of air into its big scaly chest and
with a tremendous ROAR . . .

SPLAT!
The force of the blast knocked me off
my feet!

Lying on the floor
I opened one eye
and looked around. I
expected to see fire
or scorch marks,
or at least feel
my woolly hat in
flames on top of my head.

SLIMY GOO!

But there was nothing.

Well, not *exactly* nothing. As I reached
up to my hat I felt something warm and

URGH!

sticky and slimy!
'URGH!' I
said, pulling the
slimy hat off my
head.

I looked up at
the dragon. Its eyes

were watering and more of the sticky
goo was dribbling down its nostrils. It
sniffed and looked very sorry for itself.

The dragon hadn't tried to scorch me
– it had *SNEEZED*!

SNIFF

Standing up I pulled off my scarf and

wiped the dragon's nose (I already had a slimy hat so I thought I might as well have a slimy scarf to match). Then, with a great big sigh, the dragon sniffed and flopped into a heap again.

Suddenly I heard footsteps coming down the stone stairs and echoing through the basement. The dragon's ears pricked up and its massive spiky tail started wagging excitedly.

'Daddy's home, Tinkerbell, and he's brought you some . . .' Mr Knight froze to the spot when he saw me standing

 next to the dragon and his mouth dropped open. He was obviously too shocked to speak so I thought I'd better say something.

'Tinkerbell?' I said with a smile.

'Er, yes,' said Mr Knight, rubbing his chin thoughtfully. 'She's my, er, dog.'

'Dog?' I said, patting the dragon's massive scaly belly. 'Lizard would have been a bit more believable.'

'L-lizard? Er, yes, exactly!'

he stammered. 'She's a lizard. A *really big* lizard.'

I frowned at Mr Knight.

Grown-ups always think kids are stupid and that we'll believe anything they say just because they're bigger than us. Well, Tinkerbell was bigger than any grown-up and *much* bigger than a lizard, which meant she was *definitely* a dragon.

'Shouldn't you be in class?' the caretaker said quickly, trying to change the subject. 'You could be in a lot of trouble for not being in class, you know . . .'

'Mrs Grump sent me to find out why the heating isn't on,' I said. 'But you weren't here and I found your *dragon* instead. I think she's got a cold.'

Mr Knight's
shoulders slumped.

'OK she *is* a
dragon, but she's
not dangerous.
And I only left
her to get some
cough medicine.'

He sighed, holding up a carrier bag
filled with small brown bottles. 'It's the
reason there's no heating. Tinkerbell
usually fires up the furnace.'

'The school is heated by dragon fire?'
I gasped.

The caretaker nodded guiltily.

'COOL!' I said.

'Exactly! That's the problem,' said
Mr Knight. 'Now she's caught a cold

Tinkerbell can't heat the furnace, so the boiler is *cool*. And if I can't make her better people will come down here to investigate and . . .' He looked sadly at the snivelling dragon.

'Then we'd better make her better,' I said.

'We?' said Mr
Knight with obvious
relief. 'You mean
you're not going
to tell Mrs
Grump?'

'No way!' I said.
'Mrs Grump would probably torpedo
Tinkerbell on sight!'

'Torpedo?' said the
caretaker.

'Oh, it's a long story,'
I said.

Mr Knight gave
Tinkerbell the medicine,
while I filled a bowl
with boiling water
and put a towel over
the dragon's head so she

could breathe in the steam.
That's what Mum does when
I have a cold and it always
works.

My cat Fatty had a
cold once, but instead of
being cute and helpless
like Tinkerbell, he
scratched anyone who came near him
and deliberately blew his nose all over
my duvet.

I'd *definitely* rather keep a dragon than
a cat!

'Where did she come from?' I asked, half curious and half wondering where I could get a dragon of my own.

'The egg was in the Knight family for generations. My great-great-great-great-great-great-great-great-grandfather was a proper medieval *knight* in shining armour,' said Mr Knight proudly. 'Anyway, I left the egg by the boiler completely by accident — and a few weeks later it hatched and out popped Tinkerbell!'

'Wow!' I said, thinking that my boring ancestors probably just made cakes.

After the medicine and the steam

Tinkerbell perked up straight away, her eyes brightened and she started flapping her wings enthusiastically. The dragon sat up and took a huge sniff through newly unblocked nostrils.

GRRRRROOOOOWWWWL! went the dragon's belly.

Mr Knight's eyes suddenly grew wide with panic.

'Quick, we need to get her to the furnace NOW!' he yelled, running

behind Tinkerbell and trying to shove
the big lump of dragon across the
basement. I joined him and
it took all of our strength to
budge her.

'What's wrong?' I panted,
as Tinkerbell's bottom finally
started to slide along the floor towards
the big school furnace.

'Dragons *must* breathe fire every
day or else the gas builds up and they

explode!' gasped Mr Knight. 'That's
why I taught her to fire up the school
furnace. It's the only safe place to put all
those flames.'

'And she hasn't breathed fire today?' I
said.

The caretaker shook his head gravely.

When we got Tinkerbell to the
furnace Mr Knight leapt forward and

threw the metal door open. He did it
just in time.

ROOOOOAAAAAARRRRRR!

went the dragon, as a massive jet of
flames shot from her mouth. The
furnace glowed red and the hot water
immediately bubbled in the boiler,
whooshing through the pipes that

heated the school radiators.

That was one gassy dragon!

Tinkerbell sat back looking very pleased with herself. She burped a ring of black smoke and smiled.

When I got back to the classroom Mrs Grump wasn't smiling, she was fuming (although no black smoke was coming out of her nostrils). She pointed to the clock on the wall and demanded to know where I'd been for over an hour.

'I suppose you were wandering the corridors

mrs Grump fuming!

trying to avoid lessons?' she said angrily.

'No, I wasn't! I was helping Mr
Knight with his dra–' I said, and
stopped.

If I told Mrs Grump
about the dragon she
would definitely tell the
head teacher, and
the head teacher
would *definitely* get
rid of Tinkerbell because it's probably
a health hazard or something to have
a fire-breathing dragon on school
premises.

'Well?' Mrs Grump snapped.

'I was wandering the corridors trying
to avoid lessons,' I sighed.

'Just as I suspected!' said Mrs Grump.

'Well, you'll make up for the time you've wasted during detention this evening.'

'Yes, Mrs Grump,' I said, and shuffled back to my desk.

I decided an hour of detention was

worth it. Especially if it meant the dragon could stay in the basement with Mr Knight. Tinkerbell was obviously happy living under the school, firing up the furnace every day.

After school I was sitting in detention with Mrs Grump in the nice warm classroom when Mr Knight suddenly poked his head around the door.

'Excuse me, Mrs Grump,' said the caretaker. 'Could I borrow one of your students? I have a particularly disgusting job that needs doing.'

The last time Mr Knight borrowed a student from detention they spent the whole hour scraping chewing gum from underneath the desks! Mrs Grump immediately swung her periscope-head in my direction. 'Jake Cake,' she said cheerily. 'Will you follow Mr Knight, please?'

'Yes, Mrs Grump,' I mumbled.

Outside the classroom Mr Knight was already striding down the corridor and I had to hurry to catch up with him. I was thinking it was typical – you do a favour for a grown-up and then they forget all about it!

The caretaker stopped outside the basement.

'Do I have to scrape chewing gum from underneath the desks?' I groaned.

'Hmmm,' said Mr Knight, scratching his chin. 'I suppose you can if you want. But I was thinking a *better* punishment for what you've done might be a game of Dragon Football!'

'Uh?' I said.

'Well, when I heard you were in detention I thought I'd better help you out,' said the caretaker,

making his way down the stone steps.
'And I know Tinkerbell wanted to say
thank you for letting her stay.'

As I reached the bottom step the
ground started shaking as the excited
dragon came bounding up to me and
licked my head with her
big dragon tongue.
Tinkerbell obviously
wasn't used to
visitors —
although she
soon got used
to seeing me
whenever I
got a chance
to slip away
from class.

Dragon Football is the coolest game!
The dragon is in goal and you have
to boot paper balls into the net before
the dragon can set fire to them! I wasn't
very good to begin with, but I still
managed to get a few past Tinkerbell.

It was the BEST detention EVER!

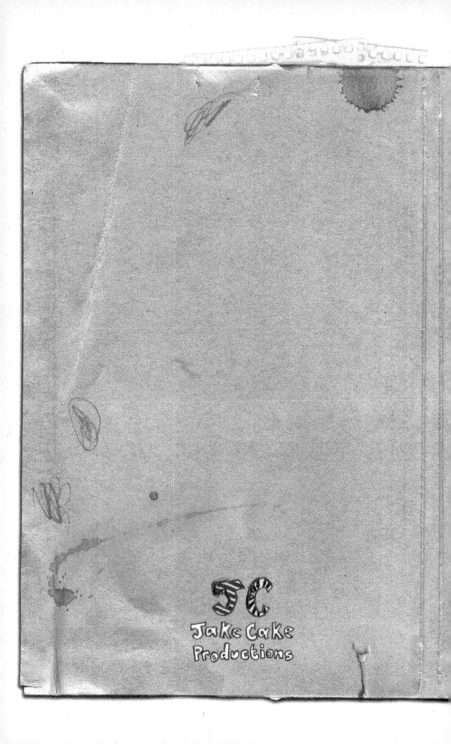

JC
Jake Cake
Productions

 TOP RIGHT THERE, ANGEL
CAKE!'

I was halfway through the garden
gate when Mum's voice boomed from
inside the house. I froze to the spot. My
first thought was that I was in trouble,

which seemed likely because
I usually *am* in trouble,
but then I realized Mum
doesn't call me Angel
Cake when I'm in
trouble so I decided not
to leg it.

Big mistake!

Still clutching the gate, I turned
round as Mum appeared at the window.
But she didn't appear at just
any old window; it was my
bedroom window, which could
mean only one thing.

'You're not going anywhere until
you've tidied up this pigsty!' Mum said.
'It looks as though a bomb went off in

here and it whiffs of smelly socks!'

Mum had been dragging rugs into
the garden, pulling out furniture and
emptying cupboards all morning.
Usually when she does a spring clean
I slope away early before she can rope
me in, but this time I'd ignored all the
signs and she'd caught me.

There was no point in
arguing, but I thought I'd

give it a go anyway.

'But . . .' I said, while I tried to think up a believable excuse.

'And no "buts" either,' Mum snapped.

I frowned and considered legging it, which would mean loads of trouble later, but Mum was already one step ahead of me. She rummaged around in the pocket of her cleaning apron and pulled out a roll of black plastic bags.

'Of course if you're too busy *I* could always clean your room,' Mum suggested casually.

Now you might think this was a good offer, Mum doing all the work and leaving me free to go out for the day. But it doesn't work like that — as I found out the last time she offered to clean my room. I came home to find six black bags being carted off by the binmen and half of my stuff missing!

Mum had won, so I sighed and slouched up to my room.

'And I don't want to see everything shoved under the bed!' Mum said, handing me the black bags and a duster. 'Not that there's any room under there anyway.'

Mum nodded in the direction of my bed and when I looked I noticed something very strange. There was *so much* stuff under my bed that

the legs weren't even
touching the floor.

I admit I'm not the tidiest person in
the world, but I've never collected *that
much* rubbish. And I was sure that my
bed had all four legs on the floor when I
got up that morning!

Our cat Fatty was lying on top of the
bed hissing at me.

FLICK FLICK

'Shoo!' I said, shaking the duster at him.

Fatty leapt on to the floor with a thud, swiped at my ankles with his claws and then sauntered out of the room. I wouldn't be surprised if Fatty had made all the mess – he'd definitely enjoy getting me into trouble.

THUD!

SWIPE!

'And I'll be checking afterwards,'
Mum said, as she made her way
downstairs. 'So you might as well do
it properly.'

I was still looking at the bed and
wondering how it had got so full
under there when I heard a small
groan and saw the whole thing move
– which made me jump backwards.

GULP!

Someone or some*thing* was
lurking under my bed.

 I suppose I could have called Mum back to investigate with me, but I didn't want her thinking I was making a fuss about cleaning my room, because then she might send me out and do it herself.

So I moved closer to the bed and poked it cautiously.

The bed quivered and I heard a tiny whimper from whatever was hiding there. I decided a whimper

was better than a growl or a roar, so I
crouched down and peered underneath.

All I could see was a pile of books
and clothes and stuff, nothing capable of
making a tiny whimper. Then I looked

closer and saw
two large eyes
peering out
at me from
behind the
pile.

GULP!

But this time it wasn't me who made
the 'GULP!'.

It came from the thing beneath the
bed.

'Hello?' I said, thinking that the thing
being afraid of *me* was much better than
me being afraid of *it*. 'My name's Jake,' I
added. But it didn't respond, so I leaned
closer to get a better look.

Suddenly the bed jerked backwards
and the pile of stuff avalanched down

to reveal a small and very frightened-looking troll with my bed still balanced on its head!

I've dealt with trolls before and there are two kinds.

There are dwarf-trolls who are small and particularly nasty (you don't want

to encounter a dwarf-troll if you can help it), and then there are bridge-trolls who are big and stupid. Bridge-trolls live under bridges (which is how they got their name), but apart from eating the odd goat, they're pretty harmless.

This troll was about the size of a dwarf-troll, but it was definitely a bridge-troll because it had horns, and a very stupid look on its face. Then I noticed it was clinging to one of my old stuffed toys and I realized it had to be a baby (because fully grown ones are massive).

But how did a baby bridge-troll end up under my bed?

By the way, this wasn't the first time

I'd found something strange under my bed. A crocodile once set up home there, and I only discovered it when I caught it sneaking out in the night to drink out of the toilet. The crocodile nearly wrecked the house when I chased it out, and I got into loads of trouble (but I'll tell you about that another time).

This time I wasn't planning on getting into *any* trouble, so I backed slowly out of the room, closed the door, and went straight downstairs to get Mum.

Because if Mum saw the troll for herself
there was no way I could get the blame
for whatever happened next.

Although she didn't take the news as
well as I'd hoped.

'A TROLL?' Mum yelled, switching
off the vacuum cleaner angrily.

'Yes, *honestly*,' I pleaded, tugging
her arm to make her come and see for
herself. 'It's under my
bed right now, in fact
it's *wearing* my bed for
a hat!'

'I'm far too busy today to listen to your stories,' Mum protested as I led her reluctantly up the stairs and across the landing. 'And if you think you can get out of cleaning your room by inventing monsters then you've got another think coming!'

I opened the door to my bedroom and nudged Mum inside.

'ARRRRRGGGGGGHHH!' she screamed.

I was feeling pretty pleased that I'd finally proved Mum wrong. But when I followed her in I noticed the

oops!

troll wasn't actually in the room any more, which meant she was screaming at something else.

Mum was screaming at the state of my room. The bed had been tipped over and the avalanche of stuff had been scattered all over the place as though something big and stupid had charged through at high speed.

'You've been up here for less than five minutes and you've already managed to make it worse!' Mum screamed. 'What do you have to say for yourself?'

'But it wasn't me, it must have been the tr—'

'And if you say "a troll did it" you'll be in *very* big trouble!' Mum growled.

There was nothing I could say to explain the blitzed bedroom that didn't contain the word 'troll' so I just shrugged helplessly. Mum went back downstairs in a very bad mood and I was left with a room that looked like it had been turned upside down.

So much for staying out of trouble!

I checked under all the rubbish to make sure the troll had definitely gone when it occurred to me that it couldn't have left the house without passing me on the stairs – which meant it was still hiding somewhere.

I tried the bathroom first (just to make sure it wasn't getting a drink out of the toilet), and when I found it empty I was immediately struck with a terrible thought. If the troll wasn't in my room,

and it wasn't in the bathroom,
that only left one place.

Mum and Dad's room!

I opened the door carefully and
peered inside.

Mum and Dad's bed was up in the
air and there were two big troll feet
sticking out of the bottom. Fatty was
sitting on top of the bed again scowling
at me, but I ignored him and leaned
down to look underneath.

TROLL FEET!

From beneath the bed two familiar frightened eyes peered out at me.

It was then that I realized the baby troll was probably looking for a *bridge* to hide under, because that's what bridge-trolls do. And when it couldn't find one I guessed it thought having a bed on its head was the next best thing.

I reached under the bed carefully and patted the troll's hand to reassure it, which was pretty scary because even though it was only a baby, it was still *well* big enough to squash me.

PAT
PAT

The troll chuckled and started
bouncing up and down,
which made the
floorboards creak and
shake like an earthquake.
I looked around the room at Mum's
perfume bottles and ornaments, holding

 my breath as they
rocked backwards
and forwards on the
rattling dressing table.
The baby troll was
a mess-making time
bomb waiting to go off!

mum's perfume bottles!

I had to get the troll out of Mum and
Dad's bedroom before it wrecked the
place and, as the first perfume bottle
toppled off the dressing table and
smashed on the floor, I knew I had to do
it fast.

My eyes fell on my old
stuffed toy in its hand.

'*Here goes nothing!*'
I whispered to
myself.

Grabbing the toy, I legged it out of the room, on to the landing and down the stairs as fast as I could. I hadn't gone far before I heard the smash of ornaments and perfume bottles, quickly followed by heavy footsteps charging across the landing and crashing down the stairs after me.

'ARRRRRGGGGH!' I yelled, because it was pretty scary.

You might wonder why Mum didn't come to find out what the racket was, but she was still busy vacuuming downstairs and couldn't hear because she was making quite a racket herself.

Without looking back I ran through
the kitchen and out into the garden.

My plan to get the troll out of the
house hadn't really gone further than
that. So when I turned and saw the

LOBBED!

troll burst
through the
back door
after me, I did the only
thing that felt right.
I kept on running!
I ran across the garden, jumped over
the fence and into the woods at the
back of the house, and kept on running
through the trees. I glanced back again
to see the troll still behind me with its
hands outstretched.

I quickly lobbed the stuffed
toy back over my head,
hoping the big baby would
stop chasing me, but
the troll caught it and
kept on running.

Eventually the trees thinned
out and I ran down the hill
towards the river.

I considered jumping in to
get away, but then realized
that if trolls live under bridges
they're probably used to water, and
can most likely swim better than me.
(I'd only just got my
100-metre badge
– which wasn't
enough to race a
bridge-troll!)

Then it hit me.

What does a baby bridge-troll want more than a stuffed toy, and more than the boy who ran off with the stuffed toy?

A bridge!

I ran along the riverbank until eventually I saw a bridge up ahead. I sprinted towards it, putting a bit of distance between me and the troll, and when I got there I stopped and tried to catch my breath.

I was so busy keeping my eye on the baby troll charging towards me that I didn't notice a huge dark figure climbing out from beneath the bridge.

not very Good
Drawing of a
↓ bridge

It was only when I saw a tall dark shadow stretched out before me that I turned and saw a fully grown adult troll looming over me, looking very, very angry. I already mentioned that bridge-trolls are stupid and harmless (unless you're a goat). But then it occurred to me that some bridge-trolls could be *so* stupid,

← SCARY TROLL- SHAPED SHADOW!

they wouldn't know the difference
between a goat and a person!

I glanced back along the bank and saw
the baby troll was almost on top of me.
Literally almost on top of me, because
when it was just a few metres away it
leapt into the air and launched itself in
my direction.

I had nowhere to go, with one troll behind me and one almost on top of me. I covered my eyes and screamed at the top of my voice.

But nothing happened. I didn't get squashed or squidged or splattered! The troll jumped right over my head!

After a few seconds I peeped out through one eye and saw the baby troll in the arms of the big troll. And looking closely I realized the big troll was female because she

was wearing lipstick (usually it's hard to
tell with trolls because they all pretty
much look the same).

'THANK YOU MUCH!' boomed the
big troll. 'YOU BRING BACK!'

'Uh?' I said, looking up helplessly and
trying my best not to look like a goat.

'BABA GOT LOST CHASING
FLUFFY IN WOODS,' she added.

'Oh!' I said, suddenly realizing
I'd led the troll home to its
mum. 'What's a fluffy?' I
asked, although I probably
should have been running away while I
had the chance.

'FLUFFY MEOW!' boomed the troll,
pointing to
the stuffed
cat in the
baby troll's
hand.

Trolls have a very
limited vocabulary, but
now I knew *exactly* how
the troll had ended up
under my bed. Fatty
had lured it there!
Which definitely
made me think he had
probably lured the crocodile there too!

That cat really doesn't like me!

The troll's mum did look pleased
to have her baby back, and as she
made her way back under the bridge
I remembered the chaos I'd left back
home. I wondered what sort of
welcome I'd get from *my* mum.

GULP!

I took my time going through the

woods back towards the house, and as I climbed the fence back into the garden I caught an unmistakable whiff of bedroom. But it wasn't the whiff of smelly socks from *my* room – it was the smell of smashed perfume bottles from Mum and Dad's room.

GULP!

The smell grew stronger as I approached the house and I could

already hear Mum yelling and making a fuss upstairs. But as I climbed the stairs and walked along the landing I heard another noise. A screeching, hissing, yowling noise, and it was coming from the bathroom.

I poked my head round the door and saw Mum leaning over the bathtub, covered in soapsuds, wrestling with

a very angry Fatty. Mum looked up and sighed at me.

'Oh, good, you're back,' Mum sighed. 'You'll never guess what Fatty has been up to with my perfume bottles!'

'What?' I said innocently, as Mum lathered up the angry cat's fur with shampoo.

'He knocked them all over,' said Mum. 'And now he's covered in the stuff!'

I couldn't help laughing to myself as Fatty glared at me from the bathtub.

It didn't take long to clear up my room, and when I finished there was nothing under my bed at all. And it stayed that way for a very long time, not least because Fatty ponged too much to lure any more monsters home.

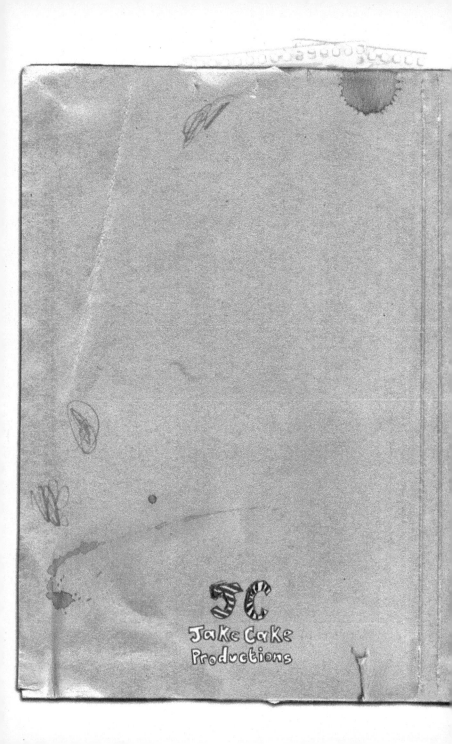

JC
Jake Cake
Productions

Apparently the Victorians lived more than a hundred years ago. Mrs Marsh, our history teacher, had been droning on about them for so long it felt like *another* hundred years had passed!

'Jake Cake!' yelled Mrs Marsh. 'Are we boring you?'

'No, Mrs Marsh,' I lied.

'Then kindly take your head off the desk and sit up properly!' she snapped, standing over me like an army sergeant inspecting her troops.

I pulled myself upright with a groan while Mrs Marsh gave me a big long lecture about how lucky I was to be able to come to school and learn lots of interesting things.

'Only very *fortunate* children could go to school in Victorian times,' she said. 'The *less* fortunate ones were sent out to work, and a boy of your age could easily find himself stuffed up a chimney!' I laughed because I thought she was joking, but Mrs Marsh got really angry.

'Some of those poor chimney sweeps *never came down again*,' she added gravely.

GULP!

I quickly sat up straight in my chair, in case Mrs Marsh decided the old school chimneys needed sweeping, when someone from behind tapped me on the shoulder and sniggered. Now you're probably thinking it was just one of my classmates mucking around. But I sit right at the back of the class, which means there *is* no one behind me!

I turned round and looked at the bare wall.

Hmmm,
I thought,
because I didn't know what else to
think.

I was still looking round when Mrs
Marsh saw me and gave me a warning
glare. And because I didn't

want to get into any more
trouble – or shoved up a
chimney – I quickly sat up
straight again and tried to
concentrate on the class.

99

I felt the tap, tap, tapping on my shoulder again, but harder this time.

'Oi! Pack it in!' I yelled, spinning round quickly to catch the tap, tap, tapper in the act. But there was no one there and no one could have run back to their seat *that* fast!

Suddenly Mrs Marsh was standing over me with a very cross look on her face.

'What is it now?' she demanded.

'Someone tapped me on the shoulder,' I said. But I probably should have made something up instead because the whole class was looking at me as if I'd gone mad.

'And who do you suppose tapped you on the shoulder?' Mrs Marsh asked, glancing at the empty space behind me. 'The Invisible Man?'

The rest of the class giggled at her joke.

'Or perhaps it was Mr Nobody?'

she said with a puzzled look on her face.

I shrugged helplessly and the class giggled even louder.

Mrs Marsh shook her head and began to make her way back to the front of the classroom when a very strange thing happened. The sharp pencil that was sitting on my desk floated up in the air, shot forward and jabbed my teacher firmly in the bottom!

Mrs
Marsh's
Bottom

JAB!

'OWWWWW!' she yelped.

Mrs Marsh snapped round, spotted the sharp pencil that had dropped back down on my desk and her eyes slowly widened.

'But . . .' I said.

'Not another word, Jake Cake!' Mrs Marsh growled. 'Take yourself to the head teacher's office immediately and explain to Mr Barton *exactly* why I've sent you there!' She snatched the pencil and held it up to eye level.

'And I'll be keeping *this* as evidence!' she added.

There was no point in arguing. Even *I* would have thought I'd jabbed Mrs Marsh in the bottom – if I didn't already know I hadn't. So I left the classroom with my head hung low and made my way down the corridor to the head teacher's office. And I took my time because I wasn't in any hurry to get there.

HE
HE

'He he,' said a voice behind me.

I stopped and looked around the corridor but there was no one there.

'He he,' said the voice again, although closer this time.

'Who's there?' I demanded.

A finger tapped me on the shoulder and when I turned round there was a

boy standing beside me, and he was grinning. The boy was about the same age as me but he was wearing very strange clothes.

''Ow d'ya do?' said the boy.

'How do I do what?' I said, not knowing what he meant.

''Ow d'ya do?' said the boy again.

I frowned and scratched my head.

'I say "'Ow d'ya do?",' said the boy.

'And then you say "'Ow d'ya do?" back.'

''Ow d'ya do?' I said uncertainly.

'Very well, thanks for askin',' he said, tipping his cap. 'And y'self?'

I considered his question for a moment and then got very angry.

'NOT *VERY WELL* THANKS TO YOU!' I yelled – realizing this kid was somehow to blame for jabbing Mrs Marsh in the bottom with my pencil (although I still wasn't sure exactly *how* he did it).

'Aw, I was just 'avin' a bit of fun!' said the boy.

'But how did you . . .'

I stopped because I suddenly noticed that, besides wearing strange clothes *and* talking in a funny way, the boy was also *definitely* a little bit see-through! I made a few quick calculations in my head and then, instead of carrying on with what I was saying, I said: ARRRGGHH!

Because that's what you're meant to do when you realize you're standing in an empty corridor having a conversation with a GHOST!

I've dealt with ghosts before and
when you scream they usually disappear
(or *you* disappear because you've legged
it in the opposite direction). But instead
of disappearing, the ghost boy just
frowned at me.

''Ave you finished?'
he said calmly.

'Uh?' I said.

''Ave you finished
screaming?' said the
ghost.

'Um, yes,' I said, feeling
a bit silly because he
wasn't actually scary.

'Good,' said the ghost.
'Well, at least you
didn't scarper. I don't

know why but most people usually
scarper when I show m'self to 'em,
which is very rude if you ask me.'

'They probably scarper because
you're a ghost!' I said. 'You *do know*
you're a ghost?' I added cautiously,
because sometimes ghosts don't
even realize they're ghosts, and
that can get really confusing.

'Of course I know!' said the ghost. 'How else could I poke a teacher in the bottom with a pencil without getting caught?'

'But Mrs Marsh thinks *I* did it!' I said angrily. 'And now I'm in deep trouble!'

The ghost shrugged his shoulders in a way that meant he didn't really care.

'You can't just get away with it!' I said. 'It's not fair!'

'I can do whatever I want,' snapped the ghost. 'And I *will* get away with it because I've been getting away with it for over a hundred years.'

'Over a hundred years?' I gasped. 'Does that mean you're a Victorian?'

The ghost thought about it for a moment.

'Well, Queen Victoria was on the throne when I was alive,' he said. 'So yeah, I suppose I am.'

'Were you a chimney sweep that never came down again?' I asked, because he did look pretty scruffy.

'No!' said the ghost who seemed a bit offended. 'I was a young gentleman!'

'So you were one of the *lucky* Victorians who went to school?' I asked, and thought that Mrs Marsh would be pleased that I'd remembered her lecture –

or at least she would have been pleased
if her bottom wasn't so sore!

'Lucky? I don't think so!'
said the ghost. 'This place
was a lot stricter in those days!'

'You went to *this* school?' I gasped.
I hadn't realized it was so old.

The ghost nodded.

All of a sudden I heard footsteps
coming down the corridor. The ghost
boy heard them too
because he winked
mischievously
and then
vanished into
thin air!

Vanishing into
thin air!

The footsteps belonged to Mrs Price, the head teacher's secretary. She was heading towards me with a stack of grey folders.

'Jake Cake!' said Mrs Price, who knew me because I've been sent to the head teacher's office loads of times – mostly for stuff that wasn't my fault. 'Why are you standing around in

the corridor looking like you've seen a ghost?'

'I've been sent to Mr Barton's office,' I sighed.

'Oh, what luck!' said Mrs Price, shoving the stack of folders into my arms. 'Would you be an absolute *dear* and carry these for me? I do suffer terribly with my back.'

With an armful of folders I followed

Mrs Price, but I kept an eye out for
the ghostly troublemaker. I thought
he might jab Mrs Price in the bottom
with a pencil or try to trip me up, but I
couldn't see him anywhere. I hoped he'd
gone back to wherever he'd come from.

'Just pop them down there,' said Mrs
Price, nodding to her desk. 'And I'll tell
Mr Barton you're here . . . *again*.' She
smiled and disappeared into the head
teacher's office.

I was about to put the folders down
when the ghost boy suddenly appeared
in front of Mrs Price's desk. I suppose
I could have just gone straight through
him (he was a ghost after all). But that
would have been too creepy so I stepped
back and gasped instead.

The ghost
looked at me.
Then he looked
at the neat stack
of folders in my
arms.

Then he smiled,
narrowed his
eyes, and
ran straight
through me
and out the
other side in
a WHOOSH of

chilly wind that
sent the stack
of folders
flying up in
the air!
(By the
way, having a
ghost run straight

through you *is* very creepy. The
sudden chill takes your breath
away like jumping into
a very cold swimming
pool. BRRRRR!)

I looked up and watched
in slow motion as each grey folder
fell open above my head – showering its
contents all around
the room in a swirling
blizzard of bright
white paper.

As the last pages
fluttered to the
ground I noticed
two figures standing
in the doorway,

staring at me with their mouths open.
But neither of them was the
ghost boy. They were Mrs
Price and Mr Barton.

GULP!

At this point I would usually
take a deep breath and explain
that none of it was my fault. But I was
the only one standing outside the office

and I'd been holding the folders. No one would believe a sneaky spook had run right through me, blasting the folders with a ghostly wind.

So I said nothing.

Mrs Price sank to her knees, gazed sadly at the fallen files and began slowly gathering them together in a pile. In the meantime Mr Barton had grown very red in the face and looked like an angry tomato.

The head teacher must have been too angry to speak because he just lowered his head and pointed towards the door to his office.

I've seen the inside of the head teacher's office *many* times, but I'd never seen Mr Barton looking so cross. He sat at his desk grinding his teeth together as though struggling to work out a big enough punishment for me.

Mrs Marsh was called to the office to give her account of *The Jabbing* (which is what they

were calling it). And because there was nothing I could say that anyone would believe, I just stared helplessly at the carpet as my teacher waved the pencil in the air like a sword – eagerly demonstrating the jabbing motion.

The last time I was in the head teacher's office was when a baby dinosaur chewed up my homework. Mr Barton had given me a big long lecture

about making up stories that aren't true
(even though I didn't make it up – it
really happened, but I'll tell you about
that another time).

This time Mr Barton must have been
thinking up a *really* long lecture because
he didn't say a word after Mrs Marsh
left the room. He just grimaced at the
pencil on the desk.

Around the walls of
the office were loads of
photographs of all the old head teachers
and they were quite fun to look at
because the old ones had freaky hair and
weird-shaped moustaches – even the
women!

The oldest one there was called Mr
Cane and the picture was so old it was

a kind of
brownish-
yellowy
colour.
Mr Cane
definitely
had the dodgiest
moustache and looked
very fierce.

I was still looking
around the room when a familiar figure
suddenly appeared behind Mr Barton's
chair. It was the ghost boy and he was

grinning and waving at me. He must
have been in the room the whole time,
probably enjoying how much trouble I
was in.

'Well, well,
well,' said
Mr Barton,
finally looking
up from
the dreaded
pointy pencil. 'Is there anything you
would like to say about *The Jabbing* before
I decide upon a suitable punishment?'

I shrugged my shoulders and tried to
ignore the sniggering ghost boy – who
was now making faces at me – when my
eyes fell on the old portraits again. It
was then that I noticed the dates at the

bottom and suddenly had
an idea.

It *was* a long shot,
but a long shot is
better than no shot at all!

'I do have one thing to
say,' I said quickly,
turning back to Mr
Barton.

'Yes?' said the head teacher, raising his
eyebrows. 'Speak up, boy.'

It was just as well Mr Barton said
'speak up', because
that was exactly what
I planned to do. I took
a massive deep breath
and yelled at the very
top of my voice.

MR CANE 1880-1914

'MR *CAAAAAAAAANE*!!!'

I have to say it was pretty loud, *so* loud that Mr Barton nearly fell off his chair.

Upon hearing the name the ghost boy immediately stopped making rude faces and made one with 'GULP!' written all over it. His eyes grew wide, his mouth fell open and his face went *very* pale – and ghosts are pretty pale to begin with.

Suddenly a tall dark figure appeared through the wall. He was wearing a long black cloak and a flat black hat with a tassel on the

top. He stood behind the ghost boy and snorted through his nostrils!

It was Mr Cane, the *ghost head teacher*!

'UH-OH!' yelled the ghost boy. Then he legged it right through Mr Barton, through Mr Barton's desk

and out through the door —
immediately followed by
Mr Cane and a great gush
of ghostly wind that swept
all the papers off the
desk and up into
the air.

It all happened really
quickly, but while Mr
Barton was busy watching his second

paper blizzard of the day, I happened
to look down
— and saw that
the pointy pencil
had mysteriously
vanished.

mysterious

missing pencil

Hmmm, I thought to
myself.

But the mystery of the
missing pencil didn't stay
a mystery for long.

'OWWWWW!'
yelped Mrs Marsh
from the other side
of the door. And I knew it was Mrs
Marsh because I'd heard the exact same
'OWWWWW!' earlier, back in the
classroom.

It was the unmistakable 'OWWWWW!' of a *Jabbing*!

As the papers fluttered down and settled on the office floor, the door creaked open and Mrs Marsh stepped in, looking very startled and rubbing her bottom. She glanced at me suspiciously, gave the head teacher a puzzled look, and then rubbed her bottom some more.

'What–? How–?' she stammered, trying to work it out.

'So Jake couldn't have . . .?' added

Mr Barton, scratching his head.

'But then who . . .?' said Mrs Marsh to no one in particular.

Obviously neither of my teachers knew what to make of the ghostly goings on, because grown-ups aren't used to unbelievable stuff happening – which is probably why no one ever believes my unbelievable adventures.

So I decided to make a couple of suggestions.

'Maybe it was the Invisible Man?' I said to Mrs Marsh. 'Or Mr Nobody?'

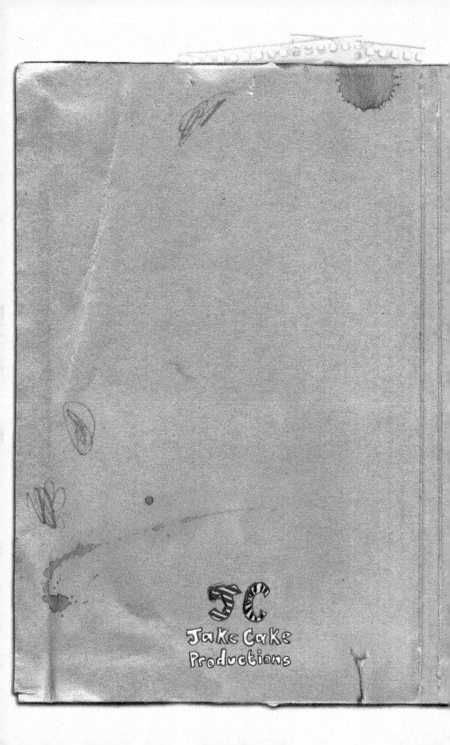

JC

Jake Cake
Productions

UNBELIEVABLE ADVENTURE REPORT

NAME: Tinkerbell (!)

AGE: Mr Knight said she's 6 years old

WEIGHT: Quite a Lot - dragons are huge!

How To Spot One. Sniff for the smell of stuff burning!

Comments: I think Dragons are BRILLIANT! They're like big ~~puppies~~ puppies with scales and they love to play games - I'd rather have a dragon than a grumpy old cat!

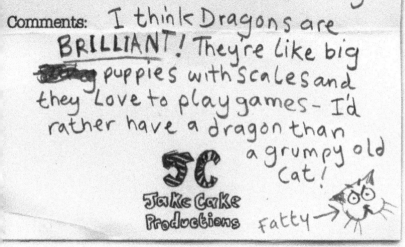

JC
Jake Cake
Productions

fatty →

UNBELIEVABLE ADVENTURE REPORT

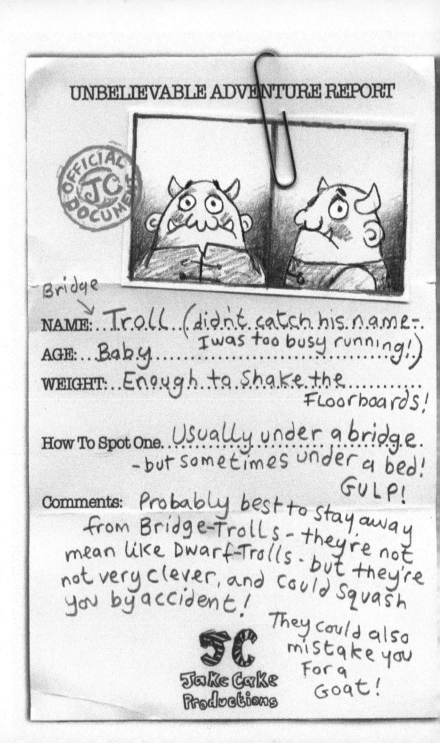

OFFICIAL JC DOCUME...

Bridge →

NAME: ...Troll.. (didn't catch his name -
I was too busy running!)

AGE: ...Baby..

WEIGHT: ...Enough to shake the............
Floorboards!

How To Spot One. ...Usually under a bridge.
- but sometimes under a bed!
GULP!

Comments: Probably best to stay away
from Bridge-Trolls - they're not
mean like Dwarf-Trolls - but they're
not very clever, and could squash
you by accident!

They could also
mistake you
for a
Goat!

JC
Jake Cake
Productions

UNBELIEVABLE ADVENTURE REPORT

NAME: Sneaky Spook (don't know his real name)

AGE: about my age - plus over a hundred years being a Ghost

WEIGHT: Ghosts don't weigh anything.

How To Spot One. Look for someone who is a bit See-through!

Comments: The Sneaky Spook would probably have been a lot of fun if he hadn't tried to get me into so much trouble - and 'Jabbing' people in the bottom with a pencil is not a very nice thing to do.

JC
Jake Cake
Productions